AF512693

Kaashvi is very creative and imaginative. She is a keen learner. Her debut book is a racy mystery set in Paris which is described beautifully by her. I wish her all the best in her future endeavours.

Ms. Kanchana Banerjee

Bestselling Author

THE LOST SOULS

THE LOST SOULS

Lost herself to find her

KAASHVI JAIN

Anecdote
Publishing House
For the love of quality reading!

Anecdote
Publishing House
For the love of quality reading!

Anecdote Publishing House
2nd Floor 2/15 Lane no. 2 Ansari Road, Daryaganj-110002
Email: info@anecdotepublishinghouse.com
Website: anecdotepublishinghouse.com

Published by Anecdote Publishing House

First Edition 2025
ISBN 978-81-973806-5-5
MRP ₹ 299

Book Promoted and Marketed by Champ Readers Pvt. Ltd.
Edited by Meraki
Cover design by Rishikumar Thakur
Layout by Graphic Tailor
Printed by Thomson Press (India) Ltd, New Delhi

This book is dedicated to
everyone who is feeling lost; it's not the end
of the world. I know it's crazy but when
you zoom out on the bigger picture of life,
you'll realize that you survived everything
you thought you couldn't, so just breathe
because this too shall pass.

PREFACE

That's the secret of existence, we're all a little mad.
–Agatha Christie

Lost souls wander without direction or purpose, yet they are not alone. In their plight, they seek out things to lose themselves in, sinking deeper into the abyss of their own despair. For Ophelia, she loses herself in a case with no real connection to her. The more she learns about it, the more she becomes entangled, descending into a dangerous spiral of obsession. As her fixation grows, Ophelia distances herself further from her own path and purpose, sinking ever deeper into the abyss.

rest in
peace

CHAPTER 1

"Whenever you get scared, run to me," my grandmother used to say this to me every time I told her how scared I was of the ghosts. The ghosts who I once believed were semitransparent creatures with grotesque appearance.

I was so naïve, so stupidly naïve.

They were always there *among me*, *among us* and they were neither semitransparent nor carried a grotesque appearance. In fact, they looked like me and you.

And now I was surrounded by too many ghosts but no one to run back to because my Grandmother was dead.

"For Christ's sake Ophelia, mute your phone," Felicia, my sister nagged at me annoyingly. I sipped the dregs of my Seltzer and apologized, "I'm really sorry, I had applied for a couple of jobs in the city so it must be them."

She sighed before she crossed her arms and attempted to glare at me. Before she could reply, our mother entered the room with a tray full of shaking cups in her hands. It seemed as though she had been crying, her hair was a mess and strands of her hair were sticking out while her face had streaks left by tears in addition to the puffiness under her eyes.

Exactly 20 hrs ago my grandmother passed away in her sleep, it was inevitable given her age but it was shocking for us all. The warm house which always radiated warmth and liveliness was now eerily quiet and empty like a void. Friends, family, relatives far and near came together to honor her memory. The room was mostly buzzing with people talking in a hushed tone about the memories they had with her.

"Let's go, the service is beginning soon." Felicia tapped on my shoulder and then got up to leave.

"Go ahead, I'll be there in a minute."

"Oh my god, can't you just switch off that phone for like 15 minutes?"

"Okay, okay geez, fine, calm down."

Defeated, I kept my phone inside my bag and followed Felicia to the living room where my parents were.

As the service began, everyone gathered in the living room, nothing but the sound of shoes hitting the well-polished floor could be heard paired with whispered conversations and then, the room fell into pin drop silence.

Slowly people took turns to bid their goodbyes and shared their fondest memories of her.

Soon relatives and friends started giving speeches, *great now I felt even guiltier for not preparing one.* Just a few minutes ago one of my distant uncles gave a speech but stopped midway as he failed to hold back tears. "*She was the most extraordinary woman I have ever me*t," he said. Another woman broke down while she spoke up about how my grandmother's investment in her small business saved her. "*I owe her my life,*" she said between stifled cries.

Felicia, stood up to speak "Hey everyone!" she waited a moment before continuing as she looked around the room, perhaps she was looking for reassurance to continue so when her eyes met mine I gave her a gentle nod.

"*I just want a moment to thank each and every one of you. Your presence here means the world to me and my family. I want to express my deepest gratitude for your kindest words and unwavering support. My grandmother was an amazing person and I-I know...*" her lips trembled as she stuttered and her voice cracked, "*I know she touched a lot of lives, she was a self-made woman and donated annually to a number of charities, she was not just a grandmother to me, but a guiding light, an embodiment of love. She was one of the first people to encourage me to give my dreams a shot, without her encouragement I would have probably been working a 9 to 5 job which I hated. I'm sure she would be happy to see you all gathered here, thank you, really from the bottom of my heart, as we say our final goodbyes, let us remember the legacy she left behind and let us honor her memory by embodying the love, kindness, and strength she showed us. May she rest in eternal peace.*" She ended her speech and took a deep breath before coming back to sit next to me.

"Great speech Fel, are you okay? You can talk to me," I said while I gave her a faint smile in order to console her to some degree at least, she just nodded and attempted to smile back at me.

Following Felicia, a woman whom I didn't quite recognize but assumed was probably one of my grandmother's friends stood up and spoke about the time she went to India with my grandmother. She spoke about how eager my grandmother was to try all the different types of foods and how she mingled well with the locals. She added about all the murder mysteries my grandmother loved to read and talk about, looking back at it I think my love for true crime and murder mysteries started because of my grandmother.

My grandmother owned a humongous library at her house and I'd get lost in the books immersing myself in each page. She would ask me about the books I had read and I narrated long summaries to her, it was kind of our thing and I would really miss it. As I sit here thinking about it, a smile crept across my face.

I will forever cherish the bond I shared with her. Even though she isn't here anymore, I'll carry the parts of her she gave me with care. I'll visit them each time I come across something that reminds me of her in the smallest ways possible because in the end that's all that matters, doesn't it? That it happened, maybe she isn't here anymore but the bond was real, she was here and I was too.

I decided to not to give a speech because I wasn't able to prepare one since the funeral was really unexpected and I caught the first flight I could get. I could sense that my parents and sister were quiet displeased by my decision but they kept quiet since they knew right now wasn't the right time to scold me for being careless.

It was really not my fault, because writing had never been my strong trait. As the mourners slowly dispersed, the room transformed into a hushed anticipation as it was time to read my grandmother's will.

A stoic figure stood at the very center of the room, he held a briefcase in hand and his greasy hair was painted blond, he was dressed in a black button up paired with black pants. He cleared his throat and began, "Since all family members are present we may continue."

"I, Barbara Cooper, being of sound and body declare all my possessions, be disposed off as follows."

I could feel the atmosphere shift; it was almost uneasy how all these people could switch from mourning the death of a person to discussing the possessions the person left behind in seconds.

"To my son, Paul Cooper, and my daughter-in-law, Lacy Cooper, for years of loyalty and dedication towards my care and for never failing to make me feel loved, I leave a sum of one hundred and fifty thousand dollars."

"To my oldest Granddaughter, Felicia Cooper, I leave fifty thousand dollars along with my secret recipe book which I know she has been dying to get her hands on."

I swore I could almost see a faint smile on my sister through her tears because of the last remark.

Felicia and grandmother had a complex relationship, they loved and cared for each other, but they never got along too well and were always bickering about one thing or the other. The only thing they seemed to have in common was a shared love for cooking. Felicia had continued this passion and had opened her own Italian restaurant in uptown Marseille called les croissants au boulevard. Even though she had access to the best recipes and ingredients, she really wanted to get Grandma's recipe book. It had been passed down to my grandmother by her grandmother, everyone knew she would give Felicia the recipe book eventually but grandmother always joked about how she will take it with her to the grave.

"To my youngest Granddaughter, Ophelia Cooper."

The lawyer looked at me and I tilted my head lightly to glance back at him with a mix of emotions of curiosity and grief.

"I leave to her my home, in Paris."

CHAPTER 2

In the summer of grade 6 when I was 11, my mom fell really sick and had to be admitted to the hospital and so I had to stay with my grandmother for a month. Felicia was already 16 so by then she could manage to live on her own, so I went to stay with Grandma alone.

That summer was probably the best summer of my childhood, well…of course apart from my mother falling sick.

From the hot summer evenings to just sitting on the porch of my grandmother's house, listening to her recite stories, I remember it all too well. Back when the world was simpler and everything looked brighter.

When I closed my eyes, I could almost hear her again.

My grandmother's voice, so soft but so full of life.

It felt like too much time had passed since I heard it but not enough to forget it. And now soon, I'd be back to that house, the very same place she lived and subsequently died. The very same house where I decided that I wanted to be an artist when I grow up.

Though I know it would never be the same but I hoped her essence would linger.

As I stood there before my grandmother's cassette I reflected and remembered moments when my grandmother had helped me, there's a lot I wanted to say but it was hard for me to think right now as tears swelled my eyes and made it hard to see.

The guests had already left and it was just me and my mom in the house as of now but I didn't want her to see me cry, so I suck it up and tried to conceal my emotions as hard as I could, I had to be strong for *her.*

Grandmother, even in death you found a way to make my life better.

The unexpected inheritance was a chance for me to break free from my struggles and begin a new chapter of my life in Paris.

Who knows? Maybe I will find my love for art again in the city of love.

You see, after deciding what I wanted to do for the rest of my life, I practiced rigorously. Till the time I reached my early teen years I could already draw better than artists who were twice and thrice my age, my art teachers said I was a *'gifted kid,'* in awe of my innate talent.

My academics however...didn't quite match my artistic gifts and I was on the verge of failing half the subjects. Despite struggling in some subjects,

I worked hard and resisted. Thus, as a result I managed to pass high school with decent grades.

With a clear goal in mind I pursued my dreams by going to an art school where everyone felt I would definitely make my mark in the art industry.

They were so wrong, so incredibly wrong.

My surety of a *bright* future got shattered as real life hit me and things didn't go as planned.

I worked as an art teacher until recently. Although the reality was very different from the one I had hoped for, I didn't hate the job. Surprisingly, I found fulfilment in watching my students grow.

Plus, they were really kind and I liked talking about art with them, I could talk about art for hours.

Except a few.

I lost my job due to false allegations and the pressure of my unpaid rent only added onto the weight.

But now with this inheritance I could change everything, I now have a second chance at my dreams. A new beginning.

This inheritance could change my life,

This inheritance has changed my life.

Thoughts of sleep consumed my mind as I sealed what seemed to be the 4th box and I had to force my eyes to not shut close as drowsiness threatened to overtake me.

"God damit!!How many more freaking boxes?"

I closed my eyes and whined while looking up at the ceiling.

It took me a lot of time to decide what I wanted to keep and what I wanted to let go. I decided on keeping only those things that were necessities and leave everything else behind, including my old painting supplies.

I wanted a fresh start.

The next morning, I woke up earlier than my alarm and got ready. I opted to wear a simple beige cardigan on top of a white tee, paired with a black skirt and knee warmers.

I still had about 20 minutes to spare till I left my house so I utilized that time to soak in my surroundings, knowing it would be my last time here.

This place will never be my home again.

This is it, it's an official goodbye.

As I made my way through each room, I couldn't help but feel a bittersweet mix of emotions. Memories of the past washed over me, from moments where I believed life couldn't get any better to the devastating times when I thought my world had ended, this place had witnessed it all.

With each step, I let my fingers graze the walls, as if trying to capture the essence of the memories embedded within them.

As I entered the kitchen, I couldn't help but be transported back to that day when I sat on the floor, feeling defeated and lost after losing my job. It was the lowest moment of my adulthood when I felt my life was over.

I closed my eyes and took a long breath.

Breathe in, Breathe out.

I was ready to let go of this place which had provided me shelter for the past 5 years of my life. I checked my clock again and realized it was time to go. I quickly double checked once more to see if I had packed everything.

I walked out of the house, with a bag of mixed emotions. It was like closing a chapter of my life, bidding farewell to the place that had been my sanctuary for so long. But I also felt a surge of excitement and hope, knowing that this was an opportunity for a better life.

It was time to move forward.

The memories would always be cherished, but it was time to create new ones because what was yet to come was more important than what was left behind.

My flight from Marseille to Paris was a one and a half hour long.

But due to turbulence and other factors, I reached Paris 2 hours later and god was it absolutely beautiful and so different from what I had remembered.

From the aroma of freshly baked croissants to the two aesthetically pleasing boulevards. Every corner of every street was picture-worthy.

I took a taxi to reach my destination and I stared at my phone screen to ensure I was at the right address.

La petit Chateau, Rue de l'Amour, Paris.

***

My memories lied to me.

This apartment whose name apparently meant "small castle" in French, was even larger than I remembered. I had been here before when I was young but I didn't really remember much about it as my memories were vague.

As I stepped through the grand entrance, I was greeted by a spacious foyer and a sparkling chandelier hanging from the high ceiling. The walls were adorned with elegant tapestries depicting scenes from French history.

The large windows were almost touching the ceiling illuminating the antique furniture and the delicate porcelain figurines of famous French figures of French Revolution from Napoleon Bonaparte to Marie Antoinette.

Just when I thought my tour was over the thought of the terrace crossed my mind, with excitement bubbling within me, I hurriedly made my way towards the elevator, eager to reach the top floor.

I checked my phone as the elevator smoothly ascended.

2 missed calls from Felicia.

I would call her back once I'm all settled in.

The doors opened and I stepped onto the terrace, my eyes widening in awe at the view that stretched out before me—the rooftops of Paris spread out like a patchwork quilt.

Finding a cosy spot on a lounge chair, I allowed myself to sink into its embrace. I closed my eyes, feeling the warmth of the sun on my face, and let the gentle breeze caress my skin.

It was a moment of pure bliss, a chance to disconnect from the world and so, I sat there, surrounded by the beauty of Paris.

la petit
chateau

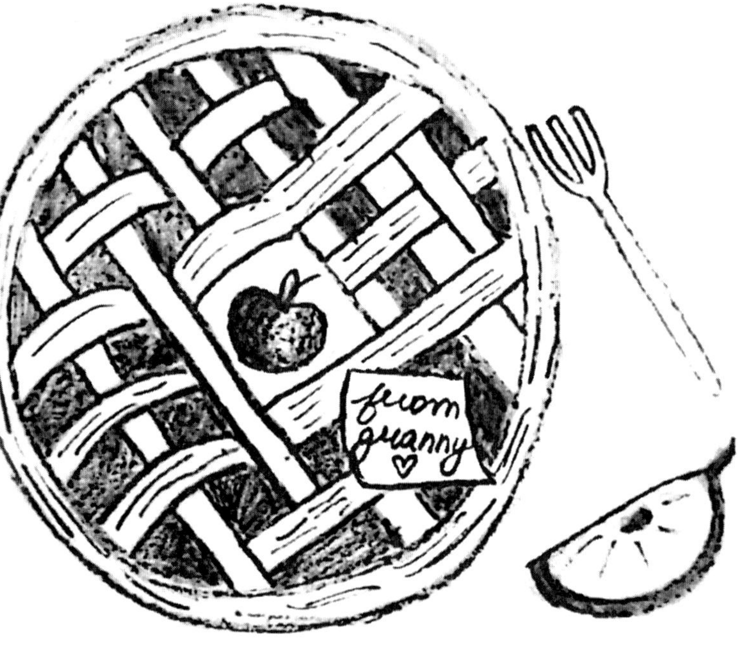
from granny

CHAPTER 3

The aroma of my grandmother's famous apple pie filled the house, adoring it with warmth and nostalgia.

"Grandma, did you cook my favourite apple pie?" I asked with an undertone of mischief.

"Yes dear, I did," she confirmed with a smile and gestured me to go towards the kitchen. I eagerly followed her actions.

As I moved closer towards the kitchen the aroma of the apple pie grew stronger filling the air with warmth and anticipation, but as I reached the kitchen, I noticed how the pie was strangely distorted. As if there was something hidden beneath its surface.

While I was looking at it, my grandmother came up behind and said in a cryptic manner, "There's more to me than you know my dear."

I looked at my grandma who had always been the embodiment of love and warmth, but now her face seemed distorted. The atmosphere changed, it suddenly became cold, really cold.

"My dear," she whispered and raised her voice to speak again.

***

I opened my eyes to my new room, the warmth of the dream replaced by the cold reality of the bedroom. The sweet aroma filled with an eerie feeling of emptiness.

I rubbed my eyes with the heels of my hands and checked the time. It wasn't even 7am yet and I didn't fall asleep until 3am yesterday, despite this I wasn't tired. I decided to get up and choose my outfit of the day.

I had just recently moved here and so I thought it would be a good idea to roam around the apartment building and familiarize myself with my new home and its people since I had some free time on hand.

Just as I got up ready to start my day, I received a call, squinting my eyes through my blurry vision trying to read the text, I saw the screen flashing...Daisy.

As I picked up the call from Daisy, I couldn't help but wonder why she was reaching out to me.

Why now?

Cause firstly, she was in no way an early bird so a call this early from her was really strange.

Secondly, we hadn't been on good terms lately but didn't have time to sort it out because we hadn't spoken in a while as our jobs kept us busy or more specifically her job treated her like a slave, giving her little to no free time but even so I picked up the call.

"Hi Ophelia"

"Hi...?"

"*Soo* I heard from Felicia you have moved cities? That's so cool! How's Paris treating you?"

"Uh Well…"

I stuttered and made a mental note to *murder* Felicia in her sleep the next time we meet. I was purposely avoiding this conversation with Daisy but now I had no choice.

"It's good. It's good, I really love it here actually."

"That's amazing, I'm really happy for you!" she tried to sound happy but I knew from the hurt in her voice that she felt betrayed that I hadn't told her about such an important thing and now we would see each other really less.

After a couple minutes of catching up, I asked her why she suddenly called me to which she replied, "Do I really need a reason to call my best friend? But anyways I heard about what happened with Mrs. Barbara and I know I haven't been a *good friend* to you recently but I still care about you and wanted to check up on you."

"It's not your fault that your job keeps you busy Daisy so don't worry about that and thanks for taking out the time to check up on me, means a lot to me, thanks."

"So how are you holding up? I quit my job *finally* and if you want or ever feel lonely, I'm just a call or text away, I swear I'll catch the first flight to Paris for you."

I laughed and replied, "Sure, but you know you're gonna have to switch off 'do not disturb' from your phone for that."

"C'mon man I was trying to be helpful," she said while pretending to be hurt.

Things felt normal between us again, I felt happy for the first time in a week. It was nice.

"But anyways Lia, how are you holding up?"

"Honestly it's the first time I'm experiencing loss so it doesn't feel like it's real yet, but every time I think of how I'll never see her again or get to eat another one of her pies my heart feels heavy, it's like a profound emptiness that refuses to leave me alone," I replied trying to stop the feeling of emptiness from taking over me again.

Daisy took a second then replied, "Grief is a part of life, and while it may feel overwhelming now, it will eventually fade away, give yourself time to heal. You're one of the strongest people I know, so don't worry and trust yourself because this too shall pass." Her advice brought a sense of peace and reassurance, and I felt grateful to have her in my life.

I closed my eyes as Daisy continued, "You know closure is not always found in the words or actions of others. Sometimes, closure comes from within ourselves, when we accept the situation and choose to move forward. You can't be stuck in the past forever, and it's not going to be easy to move on but it's not impossible either."

"Yea, thanks," I sniffed as I felt tears swell up my eyes. "Bye Daisy, I'll call you later but thanks… thanks a lot."

"What…okay. Okay, bye Ophelia, take care and remember I'm just a call or text away and I swear I'll turn off do not disturb."

"Yea, thanks and bye."

After the conversation with Daisy ended, I found myself overwhelmed by a wave of sadness. All the pent-up emotions I had been trying to bottle flooded at once like a tidal wave crashing over me. I thought I had it under control. I thought I was stronger than this. But clearly, I was wrong.

With tears streaming down my face, I allowed myself to have a much-needed meltdown. I cried out all the pent-up emotions, releasing them into the room. As I sat on the floor, surrounded by the chaos of unpacking, I knew that I had to give myself time and space to process everything I was feeling, with the first step being that I stop bottling up my emotions.

Following the much-needed mental breakdown, I got up to start my day and hopefully look for jobs nearby for art teachers because the money from the inheritance won't last forever, plus I used a lot of money to move here.

After I got ready, I prepared myself a cup of coffee, a basic necessity for every stressed artist. Feeling lighter and better after the morning crying session, followed by a hot shower and coffee; I decided to visit the rooftop, my favourite part of the apartment.

I decided to take the elevator up. It was now quarter to 8 and the sun was beginning to rise, casting a warm glow over the buildings. I found a cosy spot to sit and took in the serene atmosphere. I wished I could stay like this here forever under the sky with the sunrays hitting my face.

As I sat there in silence, it hit me that I had missed 2 calls from Felicia. I told myself I would call her back later, but I completely forgot. So, I finally decided to give her a call, but she declined. I figured she must be sleeping, so I sent her a text saying,

"Hey! I'm so sorry I couldn't call you back yesterday. I was busy checking out my new apartment. Give me a call once you read this! And by the way look at this view, isn't it the prettiest? " I attached a picture of the view from the terrace and sent her the text.

While returning back to the apartment, I got lost and ended up in the building's fitness center, perhaps this is a sign that I need to finally start doing something for my body and so I made a mental note to start incorporating exercise into my daily routine and join the center to find inner balance. Maybe this could also be the first step towards my healing.

CHAPTER 4

Following the unexpected visit to the fitness center, I headed back to the elevator. As I entered the elevator, a kind staff member gave me a warm smile so I smiled back to him. I checked my notifications trying to appear busy and avoid awkward small talk when my eyes caught a glimpse of the number 12 crossed off on the elevator button panel, I didn't remember it being there yesterday but then again, I was way too excited about the tour to notice such small things and so curiosity piqued my interest.

For a moment.

Just for a jiffy of a second.

I contemplated pressing it just for the thrill. But just as I was about to give in to my mischievous thoughts, I remembered the stranger in the elevator with me, startled, I quickly withdrew my hand and looked up at the staff giving him a nervous half-smile member, he cleared his throat and informed me, "The twelfth floor is off-limits to residents, it's under construction and not safe to access at the moment."

"Oh! I'm so sorry, I didn't mean to, I'm new here actually," I replied feeling embarrassed.

"No worries," he replied with the warm smile still plastered to his face.

***

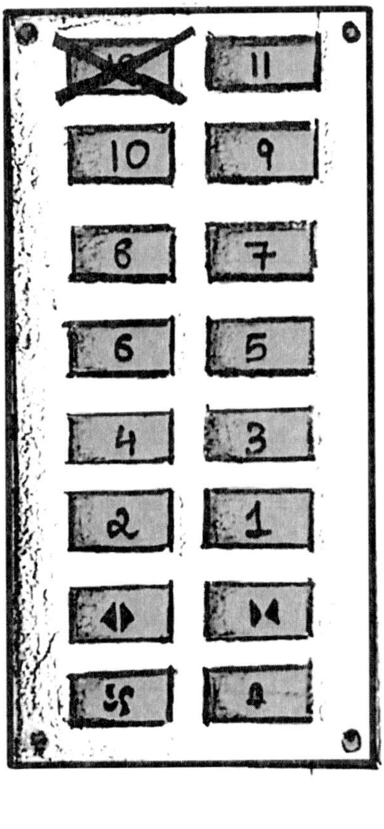
11
10
9
8
7
6
5
4
3
2
1

As soon as I returned to my room, I opened my PC and looked for jobs nearby. After about 3 hours of surfing and scrolling I found 2 decent job offers, one for an assistant in an art program and the other as a curator at an art gallery nearby. Excited about the opportunities, I wasted no time and quickly applied for both the positions.

Feeling a sense of relief, I laid down on my bed scrolling on my phone when I realized "Oh shit, I don't have formal clothes for an interview."

They say the first impression is the last impression and I had to make a good impression because I really needed this job. I decided to go shopping for appropriate formal attire. Since I was still tired because of the lack of sleep I got the previous night and the nightmare dream that forced me to wake up early, I decided to take a power nap, plus it was still only afternoon there was a lot of time left. Or so I thought.

What I hadn't kept in mind was to remember to set a freaking alarm so my power nap wouldn't turn into a 5-hour long slumber from which when you wake up you don't even remember what year it is or where you are.

So here I was at 7 pm rushing to go to the mall when people were returning from mall.

As I stepped into the elevator I absentmindedly pressed the button for the twelfth floor.

And I hadn't even realized my mistake of doing so until the doors opened revealing a dimly lit corridor which was eerily cold. Instead of being mad about it I chuckled, decided to embrace the unexpected detour. I took cautious steps forward, my senses heightened.

The air felt different on this floor, almost tinged with a sense of secrecy. As I walked down the corridor, I noticed a series of closed doors each having its own name plate, I walked along reading the various name plates.

"The Grants"

"The Martins"

"The Jains"

Oh mon dieu! this was not a construction site, this was an abandoned floor.

But as I pondered why the overly nice staff member would lie to me, my heart skipped a beat. I heard footsteps approaching.

Shit shit shit

They were growing louder with each passing second which meant whoever it was, was getting closer.

Oh god I'm not ready to die on an abandoned floor! Panic set in, and I quickly ducked behind the nearest door, hoping to hide until the coast was clear.

Please god be on my side, I swear I'll even start visiting church every Sunday!!

As I sat there I could hear the person's shoes hitting the floor, I was sure he was checking each door, I scolded myself for my irrational decisions and I held my breath, waiting for the person to check and move on.

Time seemed to stretch as I remained perfectly still, my heart pounding in my chest. Finally, the footsteps stopped but for safety precautions I stayed still.

After what felt like an infinity, I got up and let out my breathe.

That was close.

With my heart still beating in my chest, I cautiously looked around the room.

The walls were adorned with faded wallpaper, peeling in some places and a musty smell lingered in the air, adding to the eerie vibes. Dust-covered furniture stood still, frozen in time, as if waiting for someone to return and sink in its embrace. I opened a drawer and to my surprise, I discovered a…diary?

THE GRANTS
welcome

CHAPTER 5

Is it morally wrong to bring a diary from an abandoned place you just visited out of your curiosity and almost got caught at? Maybe, I think.

"What the hell did I just do," I murmured to myself while hitting my forehead with my right hand as I sat on the edge of my bed. The diary was resting in front of me, my hands itched to open it but I knew once I started there would be no going back.

I looked over the diary examining it from every angle, my fingers grazed its pink cover which was adorned with delicate white patterns.

"Pretty" was all I could say.

It was hand crafted and whoever crafted it definitely had a lot of potential as an artist.

Judging from its design it definitely belonged to a kid and probably a girl.

As I gazed over at the diary, I couldn't help but wonder about what was written inside? Who it belonged to? Where was this person now? Why was this diary lying there?

My mind was filled with questions, and I knew they would be answered if I just opened the diary.

The urge to do so was strong, but I persisted, torn between fascination and caution.

The decision was mine but one thing was clear—I wouldn't be able to hold my temptation for too long, so, with a deep breath, I made my choice. Slowly, I reached out and gently turned the first page.

Property of Krista Grant

Ps. Do not read unless given permission

I was right, it did belong to a girl, and god she had amazing handwriting. The page was decorated with pink bow stickers and the sentences were written with a black pen in calligraphy in the center of the page, so that they are the first thing that catches someone's attention. I turned the page again, this one was filled with more sentences and less stickers but it kept up with *coquette* aesthetic and pretty handwriting.

2nd March
Dear Diary,

It feels a little strange to be writing about myself, but anyways, let me take a moment to introduce myself.

Hi! I'm Krista, and it's my sweet 16 in 2 weeks. I love listening to music, in fact I have my headphones on for long periods of time every day (even as I'm writing this, I have my headphones on).

I find comfort in creating things. In my spare time, I like to draw, especially making sketches and inventing their backstories. Art makes me feel seen and alive, because when you fall in love with a piece of art, you fall in love with a fragment of another person's imagination—like that is so beautiful.

I didn't really have many friends growing up, but I'm okay with that. I enjoy being by myself, plus being with others mean I have to act in a certain way which is restricting and I already have far too much of that at home.

It's been a little overwhelming adjusting to a new environment and culture, but I'm slowly coming to terms with it. My neighbors are really kind to me, in fact yesterday an old lady baked me cookies and they were so tasty and they had chocolate filling inside which melts in your mouth once you bite into the cookie, plus I could feel the kindness she poured into her cookie. Even though it was a really small action I just thought that it was really a kind gesture.

Also, I got to go now, mom's calling me to assist her with something.

***

'Krista grant,' I whisper to myself.

I *feel like* I've heard that name somewhere.

I *know* that I've heard that name somewhere.

I put the diary on my side table and rush to get my laptop and open Google.

'I hope she's not who I think she is.' I think to myself as I press search.

It's as I feared. There's no doubt this diary belongs to Krista Grant, the girl who went missing with her family all those years ago. When I first heard the story, I was only sixteen and it stuck with me. *It haunted me.*

The idea that someone could just disappear without a trace, never to be seen or heard from again is unfathomable. It really is a reminder of the fragility of bonds, since people can disappear without a trace anytime and all they will become someone you used to know.

I looked at the journal and picked it up again, and began flipping its pages.

As I flipped through the diary, I couldn't help but experience conflicting feelings. On one hand, it's fascinating to get a glimpse into Krista's life; it's interesting to get to experience her life through her words like a little secret. But on the other hand, there's this sense of guilt and sadness, these are her words, an unfiltered version of her, something she probably never wanted anyone to read; something she kept hidden.

As I continued flipping through the pages of her journal without actually reading them, I accidentally dropped it and saw blood scattered on one of the pages.

I counted them, there were 1..2..3..4..5. There were 5 tiny droplets of blood, *real blood* turned brown by time. An eerie reminder that she was missing, no one knows where she is, no one knows how her brother died and *I have her journal.*

Something that could put an end through the Grant family mystery, a key, a link to her and her disappearance.

Could this be the missing piece of the puzzle that ties it all together?

CHAPTER 6

This is stupid, so stupid.

I should submit this to the cops, I mean *this* is hardcore evidence.

But, would they even care? They didn't care when I tried to explain to them that I didn't do it. I would never accept bribes from parents for the sake of passing their kids, but no one listened to me, I tried to explain how the evidence was fake but no one even batted an eye to my words.

They didn't care that my life was getting screwed

up because they got bribed.

They didn't care that I lost my job, something I loved, something I enjoyed doing over something I never did.

But, at the same time, what would I even be able to make use of this, I mean for sure I can't start investigating about a closed case with no prior experience in investigating, *could I?*

As my head spun with questions I realized one thing, if I could have found the journal that means the police must have too, the case was all over media. The police used all of their resources to try to solve the unexplainable death of Lucas, but then the case mysteriously got shut down and the Grant family disappeared from the eye of media only to be never heard from again.

I fire up my computer and begin a deep dive into the case, searching for anything related to this mysterious journal.

I scour through news articles, police reports, and any available information I can find but there's no record of any other evidence or clues that could link back to the journal.

Surely the police must have searched this abandoned building as well. But why didn't they find the diary? Could it be that the police overlooked something? Or is there something more sinister at play here?

It's like a mystery within a mystery. I know I found the diary in an abandoned building, but where did it come from? And why was it left behind?

The questions kept spinning in my head. Every time a new thought crossed my mind, it just raised more questions. How am I supposed to find answers if I don't even have a starting point?

I picked up the journal again from where I left off, and I noticed something new. There's a gap between her pages, she didn't write for an entire year, this page was written after her brother's death..

26th February TIME: 9:05 pm

Dear diary,

Today has not been the best. It's been exactly one day since my brother's death. Everyone wants me to move on, but how can I? It feels like one moment he was here until he wasn't. I feel empty, so empty. This loneliness is killing me, I feel so lost. He was my everything, I still remember how warm he always was, how his brightness shone through the darkest times, he was my favorite person, a safe place.

I thought everything was okay as long as I had him, but now nothing is okay and he's gone forever, he's not coming back.

My family is in absolute shambles and I don't know how to cope. It feels like we're just existing. I hate feeling this way, but I hate the fact that I'll have to move on from him; I don't want to forget him, I want to hold onto him. I know it's bad for me and unhealthy but can you really blame me?

My parents have stopped talking to each other. There's silence, the once lively family dinners have turned into awkward silent dinners. My father no longer smiles or laughs the way he used to. He's always locked up in his office making strange calls. My mother is trying her best to hold the family together but I can tell she's not okay. Things are not just the same anymore.

Now every time I look at an old photo of him with his gummy smile, my heart aches and I breakdown, he didn't deserve it, not my Luca.

I can't believe someone would do that to him, I can't believe that his killer is out there.

He saved me from so many things, but now no one could save my saviour.

YOURS TRULY,
Krista

This feels personal to me. Her words are so raw

and full of emotion, I can almost feel them. I turned another page, this one's written 4 days after the previous diary entry and is shorter.

Dear diary,

Luca got buried, I still can't process he's gone.

But isn't it weird that my dad didn't attend his burial? He doesn't even talk to me or my mom anymore. My mom just cries all the time and tells me to go away as if I did something wrong.

Marshal says it is. Oh I forgot to tell you I made a new friend, his name is Marshal and he works at my apartment. I met Marshal when he was working in the apartment building where I live. I often saw him around the hallways and common areas, and we gradually got to talking. It started off with a small chat about the weather or other small talk. Over time, our conversations began to linger longer and become more substantive.

> He has light green eyes, pitch black hair and is from the UK, so he has a British accent.

Hold on, this description sounds exactly like the guy from the morning, they were friends?

I put down the diary and open my laptop, to look at photos of Krista.

She looks so innocent and delicate, she is wearing a white dress which ends right above her knees, full arms and a pearl bracelet with alternating white and pink colors, that bracelet...I've seen it somewhere, the guy from the morning, he was wearing the same bracelet.

The description, the bracelet, It's him. He's Marshal. I got my first lead.

CHAPTER 7

My head was pounding, still recovering from the marathon session I had on my computer the day before. I dragged myself out of bed and headed towards the bathroom. I desperately needed to take some medication to help ease that headache. My body felt heavy and sluggish; like a burden I could barely carry.

After taking the pills, I sat down on the edge of the bathroom tub, waiting for the medicine to take effect. My mind was a fog and I could barely think straight. My thoughts kept drifting back to that journal and its elusive secrets. The pain in my head made it a struggle to focus.

As my headache began to subside and the pain slowly vanished I realized that I had been sitting in the bathroom for far too long and that I needed to get moving. I hopped up from the bathtub and headed out of the bathroom. As I passed the mirror, I got a glimpse of my reflection. I didn't look very presentable, with my hair disheveled and bags under my eyes.

Plus, I had an interview for which I had nothing to wear, so after taking a bath and putting on concealer to hide the bags under my eyes I threw together an old white shirt with a black blazer to hide the tea stains on the shirt along with black cargo pants. Maybe not the most appropriate outfit for an interview but it worked well.

Before leaving my room, I made sure to hide the diary in my almirah underneath my clothes, it's not like I thought someone would steal it but I couldn't trust anyone fully yet.

***

As I entered my apartment building, I felt confident about the interview, I thought it went well and I'm pretty sure I would get the job. With air pods in my ears, I entered the elevator and pressed the button for my floor.

But my mood shifted suddenly as I noticed the man from yesterday, he was wearing all black. We locked eyes and I could feel my heart beating out of my chest as I stared at him.

The silence was deafening. It felt like an eternity passed before the elevator doors finally closed. Then it hit me, but it was too late, the doors had already closed. As soon as I reached my floor, I took the stairs and run to where I had seen him, him but he was already gone.

The front desk, maybe I can get some information about him there.

I ran to the front desk of my apartment building to inquire about him. The attendant behind the counter gave me a strange look, confused by my request.

"Who is the employee you're looking for?" the attendant asked in a hushed voice.

"Does someone named Marshal works here." I asked, still breathing heavily.

"Oh, you mean Marshal the maintenance guy," the attendant nods.

I waited anxiously for his arrival, my heart rate increasing with each ticking second. I leaned up against the counter for support, still a little shaky from the encounter.

After a few minutes, I heard footsteps approaching. A man walked out from behind the corner and made his way to me.

Bracelet, he is wearing the bracelet, I was right, it's him.

"How may I help you ma'am," he said giving me a kind smile.

"Uh I—," I stutter, shit what do I say now?

"The elevators, they are very...," he interrupted me, probably sensing my anxiety.

"That's true, the elevator is very dirty and it's been a problem for some time now. I'll make sure to follow up on that right away. Is there anything else you need to tell me?" he asked while exchanging glances with the attendant.

"No, that should be all," I said while trying to find my cool.

CHAPTER 8

It would be the perfect opportunity to find out more about Krista, but I had no idea if he would be open to talking.

What should I try first? Investigating Marshal would definitely lead to more answers, if I could figure out how to pry them out of him.

He had already left but he couldn't have gone far, if I could catch up to him maybe, just maybe he would tell me something, It's worth a shot.

"Marshal wait!!" I yelled as I called him out.

"Yes ma'am, go ahead," he said politely while maintaining his kind smile.

"I actually need to talk to you about something," I said and added, "it's a little personal."

"Okay," he responded with an unsure look. "Can you say it right now or...," he spoke before I interrupted him. "Can we meet somewhere? How does the terrace sound, today at 6 pm."

"Sure ma'am," he responded still looking puzzled. "Okay good, thank you," I said then walked away.

***

It was 2:45 pm, which meant I still had 3 hours and 35 minutes left until my meeting with Marshal. I opened my laptop and started researching again, since I still didn't know much about the case.

This time though, I started researching from a different angle. I tried to think outside the box, looking for clues that might have been overlooked. I went through everything yet again, this time after analyzing every detail I couldn't seem to find anything substantial. Every news article, every video, every report said the exact same thing in different words.

I have to take matters into my own hands. If I need to know more about this mystery, I couldn't rely on the internet only.

Plus what bigger clue could I have gotten than Krista's diary?

I checked the time again, it was 5 pm, I still had an hour to go so I opened back her diary and started reading from where I left.

> Dear diary,
>
> My parents are acting weird. I'm trying to come to terms with the fact I might never know how my brother died, but they keep acting differently. They frequently ask me about what happened the night of my brother's passing, or if I remember anything, asking for more details that does not make

> sense. I think that there is something more behind his death, I mean like I just can't shake off the feeling that my parents are trying to hide something from me. I feel so uneasy, it's already so hard to cope and they keep adding more to it.

Wait, they kept asking her if she remembered anything? Does that mean she was there when he died?

What...?

And her parents kept that hidden?

This is a huge thing. I took out my notepad and started penning down questions to ask Marshal as I continued to read through the pages.

> His room is still the same as it was before, sometimes I go there and pretend he is still here. I can see parts of him everywhere but I can't find him anywhere. I still wear the bracelet he had made for me . Oh, and by the way, my parents also put me in therapy, it's a bit out of my comfort zone but Dr.

Richer is a really sweet woman, and she is nice to me and I feel comfortable with her.

Bye diary, with love,
Krista

***

I immediately took out my phone out and searched Dr. Richer Therapy and just like that, I found my next clue, her workplace was only a 25 minutes drive from here but she was closed for the next 2 days and then the entire day was booked, so the nearest appointment I could get was after 3 days. I immediately booked a session with her.

Do you wish to book an appointment?

YES	NO

CHAPTER 9

I arrived on the roof 10 minutes early, but to my surprise he was already waiting for me, the atmosphere was a fusion of eeriness and tranquility matching my current mood.

I took a deep breath. I can do this, I totally can. I started to take slow steps towards him. All I gotta do is talk to him.

"Hi marshal," I said with a wave and a smile, trying to appear friendly, while still walking towards him. He responded back with a wave and his kind smile. He smiled, that's a good sign I guess.

"So listen, before we begin I just want to say I'm so sorry for disturbing you," I said. "No worries ma'am, I'm always happy to help, so can we begin?"

"Okay, so, hi I'm actually a college student who is doing a very important project, I took Krista's case as the topic of my project and I just wanted to interview you on that."

I lied to him but that was because I couldn't have told him about the diary, I sensed a shift in his expression and so I stopped talking.

"Krista?" he whispered to himself but due to the quiet atmosphere I heard it, though I didn't say anything and maintained my smile. "You called me here to interview me about Krista?" he said this time with a mix of anger, shock and confusion.

"Why me though" he asked flatly.

"According to my research till now, you two were good friends, weren't you?" I responded.

"Your research is wrong," he said angrily then stormed off before I could say anything else.

What? I was wrong? But, when he heard her name, I could see it, he knew her, I had to take a chance and so I ran after him. "Marshal wait!!" I yelled from behind and thankfully he stopped.

"I'm sorry if that was offensive to you in any way, I'm just trying to complete my project, can I just ask you some basic questions?"

"I'm sorry but I'm not sure I would be the right person to talk to about her," he said. I took a deep breath and asked, "Then who is?" to which he responded, "Anyone but me." And started walking again.

"Wait," I yelled again and added, "please? Just 6-7 questions?"

He thought for a while and said, "Okay sure but only 3." "Deal," I said with relief.

"Okay so, let's begin," he said.

"Yea, Let's begin."

I could sense Marshal's hesitation and I was starting to get nervous myself. I wanted to get more information about Krista, but I didn't want to overstep any boundaries.

"Did she ever mention anything about her family?"

Marshal considered the question for a split second, his eyes widened slightly.

"Um... I can't recall her mentioning her family. She rarely even talked about herself at all. She was a very private person, I never knew what her personal life was like. But I do know she wasn't that close to her parents, she didn't really like them much and blamed them."

I felt a bit frustrated by his answer. But I didn't want to push him for more information. So I asked him, "Blame them for what exactly?"

"Everything that went wrong with Luca, her brother, she kind of just spiraled after his death," he responded while staring at the ceiling.

I gave him a nod, took a deep breath and asked him the next question, "Before she went missing, did you notice anything unusual?"

He told me that he did indeed notice some changes in Kristia's behavior leading up to her disappearance.

"I noticed that she had started acting strange... more withdrawn, more nervous. It was like something was troubling her, but she never made a big deal out of it."

Marshal continued, saying that he was concerned for her, he had noticed some anxiety symptoms as well, being a psychology student. He recalled that she had been having trouble sleeping due to nightmares and panic attacks, but that she had made an effort to keep them to herself.

That poor girl, she was suffering all alone.

"Did you ever find out the cause of her anxiety symptoms?"

Marshal shook his head, and said, "Krista never disclosed the source of her anxiety, just that she'd been experiencing nightmares and panic attacks."

He said that Kristia was a private person and rarely shared personal details. The incident with her brother had affected her deeply, but she didn't like talking about it.

"Okay, so thanks for all the details, let's move onto the next question?" I asked him to which he responded with a nod.

"Did you see her before she disappeared?"

"No, I didn't see her before she disappeared. But I know someone who does think they saw her."

"Who?" I asked curiously.

"It's this guy named Michael. He claimed to have seen her on the day she went missing."

"Do you have any more information about him?"

"Yeah, I do. I can provide you his address and phone number, if you'd like."

"Great, could you type it down for me?" I asked while handing him my phone which had the notes app opened. Marshal nodded and proceeded to write down a phone number along with Michael's house address on a piece of paper. "There you go." I thanked him for his time and put the piece of paper in my pocket.

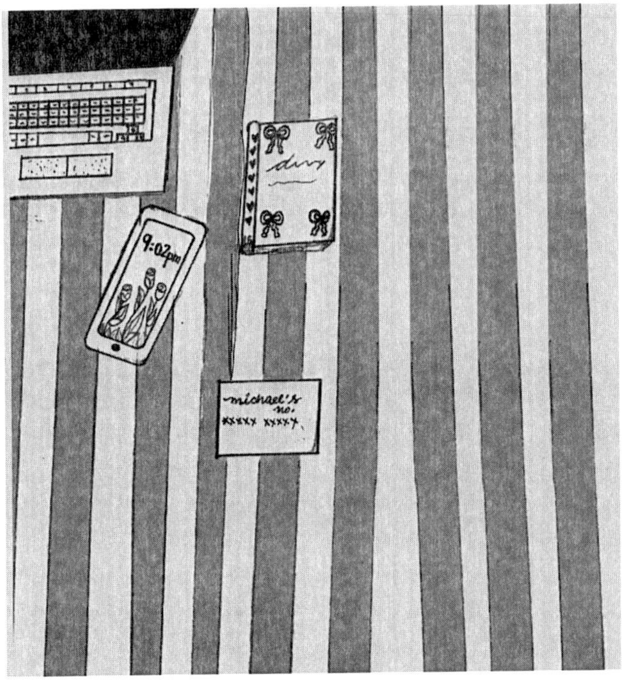

CHAPTER 10

I woke up the next morning and made my way to Michael's house. I stood outside the front door for a moment, trying to prepare myself for the conversation. I wasn't even sure what I was going to ask him about Krista but any information would be valuable.

I took a deep breath and knocked on the front door.

I waited patiently for the door to open. I could hear footsteps coming from the inside, indicating that someone was inside the house. I was starting to feel nervous as I waited for Michael's arrival.

After a few moments, Michael opened up the door, only a crack. He stared at me with a puzzled look, before finally speaking:

"Can I help you? I don't know why you're here, but I don't have any money on me if that's what you're after."

"I'm here to ask you about Krista," I responded calmly.

Michael grew nervous at the mention of Krista. He was unsure of how to respond and started to back away from the door, clearly feeling uncomfortable with the subject matter. "Hey, wait!" I called out to him but Michael continued walking, so I rushed forward and grabbed hold of his arm, halting his movements.

Michael froze in his tracks at the sudden grab of his arm. He slowly turned around to face me, his eyes filled with fear and his body trembling slightly. He looked really afraid and his eyes were pleading for me to stop asking questions, to stop prying further.

I could see that his reaction to my touch confirmed my suspicions that he knows something about Kristina.

I don't let go of Michael's arm as I stared intently into his eyes. I was determined to learn the truth about Krista's whereabouts. So I asked him the question directly.

"Did you see her on the day she disappeared?"

Michael hesitated for a moment and his eyes widened, clearly unsure how to answer the question.

I asked him again almost screaming this time "Did you see her the day she went missing?"

"Yes. Yes, I did see her. Please stop. Leave my hand. Please leave. Please please."

I loosened my grip on his arm and asked him another question completely ignoring the last few words.

"Where did you see her? And when was it?"

He hesitatingly answered, "I saw her at the park. And it was the night she went missing, just a few hours before she went missing."

I stared at Michael, feeling overwhelmed with emotions. "What was she doing at the park that late at night? It's so late, she wouldn't be walking in an empty park by herself."

Michael looked away uncomfortably, seemingly reluctant to answer the question.

I could feel his fears soothe just a bit, he relaxed a little and answered with a sad undertone.

"Honestly, I don't know. She was just walking around, or maybe she was running? I'm not sure but she was looking like she was deep in thoughts. She seemed frantic about something or maybe someone. I had stopped to sit down and smoke a cigarette when I saw her and.... I didn't think anything of it at first."

"Can you tell me exactly what she had said?" I felt an urgency as I asked the question.

"She was crying and mumbling about not wanting to go there," he said.

"Go where," I asked him now confused.

"That, I have no clue about," he said nonchalantly and added, "and before I could say anything she started running away again, that was the first and the last time I saw her till I saw her missing case on the news."

CHAPTER 11

I didn't get a lot of useful information from him but what did she mean by she didn't want to go there?

Where did she not want to go?

It was finally the day to meet Dr. Richers, maybe I could get more information there.

I walked into the office, taking a seat in front of the psychologist. She wore a crisp white lab coat that hung just below her knees. Underneath, she wore a navy-blue pleated skirt that reached just above her knees.

The psychologist welcomed me, and I felt a sense of relief. However, I also felt a sense of worry, knowing that I needed to be cautious with my conversations.

I took a deep breath and waited for the psychologist to start the conversation. The psychologist began asking me general questions, such as how I was feeling and what had brought me to seek out counseling.

As the session progressed, I got more comfortable with her, she seemed nice, she was a cheerful lady who radiated positive vibes, I took a deep breath and asked her, "Do you know Krista?"

She seemed a bit taken aback my sudden question and answered, "She was one of my previous clients, nothing else."

I could sense the change in her behavior, so I didn't pry further. I excused myself but instead of going to the bathroom, I went to the storage room.

I was breathing heavily as I searched through the

room looking for the place where they would keep old records. The place was dimly lit and confined.

Once I finally found the records, I searched through them to find Krista's file.

There weren't many files from that particular year so I was lucky enough that I wouldn't have to go through so many files.

Not this one, not that one either, I was beginning to lose hope.

I had trouble finding Krista's records. I spent more time than I expected scouring through the files, but I eventually reached the right section and found her folder.

I opened it full of hope, anything just anything, any piece of information would be fine.

It was empty.

There was nothing.

No record.

Nothing.

I checked it again but indeed it was empty. I felt frustrated, I didn't spend so much time only for this to lead to nothing.

I went back to the session, feeling frustrated after finding the empty folder. I sat back down in front of the psychologist, who noticed my agitated state and asked me what happened.

I responded to her saying I got a call and needed to head back early to which she responded with a kind smile and waved me goodbye.

***

Once I was finally home, I sank into the warm embrace of my bed, these past days had been hectic and I barely got any sleep and on top of that I still hadn't gotten a call back for my interview, and with each passing day I was losing hope. I was tired, so tired, I wanted to sleep but I wasn't able to, it was exhausting.

I did my skincare routine, using my favorite products to try to relax. After, I finished my skincare routine, I decided to relax a bit before turning in for the night. I felt mentally exhausted after everything that had happened and just wanted to take my mind off the situation.

I decided to watch a show on Netflix, but I found it hard to be engaged with the show as my mind kept wandering back to Krista.

Feeling uneasy, I decided to read one more diary entry. So, I went to my cupboard to get it from there.

It was gone, there was nothing there. Everything else was in place, except the diary.

And a note…a phone number?

What. What, what…?

I began to search for the diary, but it was nowhere to be found. I decided to check all the drawers in my room, desperately hoping that I was simply overlooking it.

I searched through all the available drawers and cupboards, still hoping to have missed it somewhere. With no success in finding the diary, I began to feel more frantic.

I decided to search other parts of my apartment but I found nothing. I started to wonder if someone had stolen her diary and who it could be.

I continued to search my house for the diary, even searching in places where I wouldn't normally keep a diary. I started to feel frustrated and anxious at not being able to locate it.

With each passing moment, that I couldn't find the diary I grew more and more anxious, worried that someone might have stolen it or tampered with it.

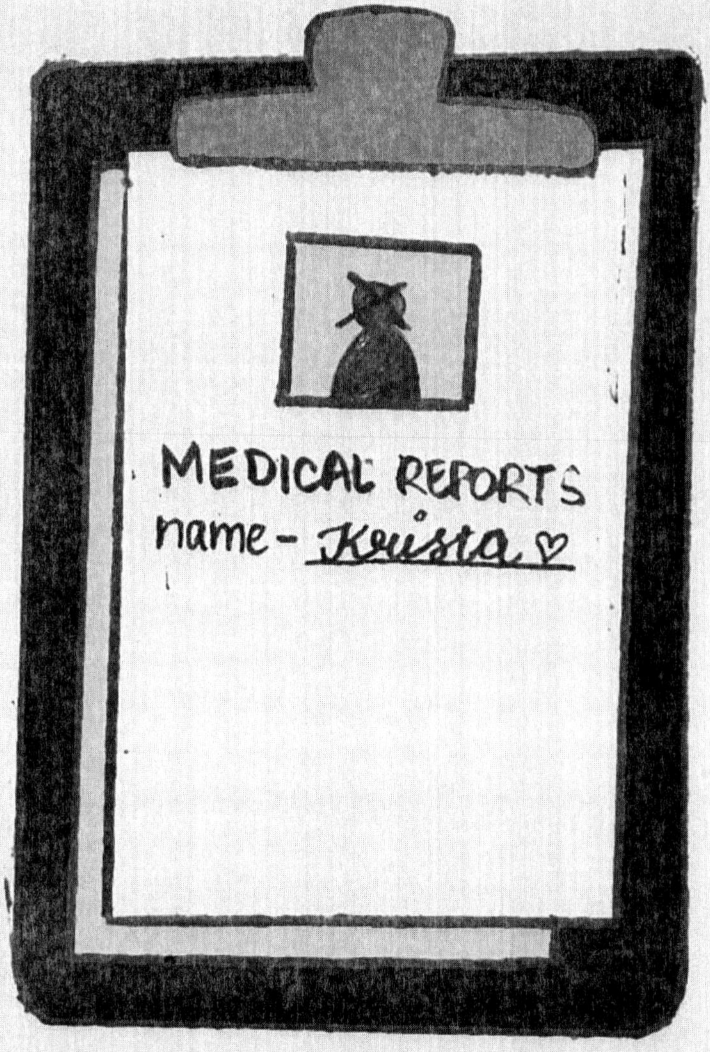
MEDICAL REPORTS
name - Krista

TO DO

CHAPTER 12

I could feel uneasiness wash over me as the realization dawned that someone had broken into my apartment.

Someone was here.

My privacy had been violated, and it was unsettling to think that a complete stranger had access to my personal space.

And most of all, they stole the diary. I didn't feel safe here, not anymore.

I had to run, but where?

Where would I go?

Just as my head was spinning with questions, I ran out of my apartment and bumped into Marshall. He could sense the anxiety, and decided to ask about my current situation. He wanted to help, but he didn't know how and he seemed more impatient than compassionate.

Marshall offered me water to help with my anxiety. I was thankful for his gesture, but the water also made me feel more anxious for some reason.

He seemed nice, right? I Could trust him, right? I didn't know but he helped me, that counts for something at least, right?

I was anxious, I needed someone to talk to so I decided to tell him about the diary. I took a deep breath—Inhale and exhale.

"Marshall?"

"Yes? Are you okay now?"

"Uh yea… um actually I need to talk to you about something."

"Sure, go ahead."

I began to explain to him everything about the diary, where I found it, the people I met, the note with the number, its disappearance, everything.

He was shocked, of course he was. But I could also see he was angry.

He looked me dead in the eye and said plainly, " Krista is dead." Then added, "Stop searching for her, she's gone."

She

Is

Gone…?

He straight out told me that I should not waste my time and start grieving. He told me that I should give up on finding Krista, as she is no more. I felt shocked by his lack of compassion.

***

I went to sleep that night with all the thoughts of Krista on my mind. I couldn't seem to be able to stop the spiral of anxiety that was running through my head every now and then.

He also told me that the number belonged to Yolanda, Krista's mother. He told me to talk to her and clarify things if I needed to.

CHAPTER 13

I woke up the next morning with the number still with me. I looked at it and felt a little bit nervous, not sure what to do next with it. I felt like I should call it but I also felt uncertain about who might pick up on the other end of the line.

For some reason I didn't believe it was Yolanda, maybe it was that I didn't want to be her.

After many moments of thinking, I finally decided to call the number, figuring I had nothing to lose at this point. I felt nervous and I held my breath as I pressed the call button. The phone rang and I waited, hoping for someone to pick up.

It took 5 rings till the person on the other end finally picked up.

I was taken back by the person who picked up, it really was Yolanda Grant.

"Hello?" I said first.

"Ophelia?" I panicked. "Am I talking to Ophelia?" she asked again.

"Yes. Yes, it's Ophelia."

"Okay," her tone dropped to annoyed, she sighed and continued, "meet me at *La Brioche Divine* tomorrow at 6 sharp." And then she cut the call. *Rude.*

I made sure to be punctual and arrive at the meeting spot 5 minutes early. I was a little nervous as I walked into the café, she was already there looking out of the window till she turned her head and looked at me.

I thought she might greet me, or at least offer a smile.

"Name your price," she said plainly. I was a bit taken aback, what price was she talking about?

"What do you mean?" I asked.

Yolanda casually ignored me and ordered a latte for herself until she finally spoke, "Why are you doing this? Who do you work for?"

"I'm not doing this for anyone and what do you even mean…"

"Then name your price so we can both save some time and you can drop your research."

"Okay first of all, I'm not doing this for anyone except myself, you can think of it as one lost soul trying to help another lost soul, now can I ask you something?" I said visibly annoyed.

"Whatever, make it quick."

"What happened that night?"

"What night?"

"Don't play dumb Yolanda, we both know what I'm talking about."

She sighed and completely ignored me.

"If you don't tell me what happened, I'll tell everyone that Krista is dead."

She spat out her coffee and looked at me with a mixture of rage and confusion.

"Shut up," she shouted. You have no idea what you are talking about, that girl was a psychopath and I'm glad she's gone."

Her expression now hinted at a mix of anger and sorrow, the corners of her eyes growing watery as she tried to hold back the tears, I think I hit a nerve. I felt bad for her now even though she just screamed at me.

So I said sympathetically, "Yolanda…It's okay you can talk to me."

"No no no you don't... you don't get it," she said frantically fast.

"That girl suffered from something called DID...? I think that's the name but I'm not sure," she started crying.

"The disorder with multiple personalities?"

"Yes. Yes, that," she continued sniffing.

"Okay...what does that have to do with anything?"

"It has everything to do with this."

"How?"

"I can't tell you but just stop okay; stop searching and researching, Just focus on your life. You have a beautiful life ahead of you. You don't know me, but I know you, you are Barbara's granddaughter"

I was a bit taken aback by her last statement but I didn't let that show, she must have researched on me, probably. Instead, I took a deep breath and continued with a stern voice

" Yolanda…if you don't tell me I'll tell everyone she is dead."

"Stop," she screamed again "You don't get it, you won't understand."

"Then make me understand."

" That girl.. she is a monster… that girl," she started sniffling and continued, "killed my son," she screamed while crying.

Krista killed Luca

PROLOGUE

KRISTA

I am stranded in a sea of unanswered questions and fading recollections. The past is drowning me. I feel heavy but weightless. The currents are pulling me down, deeper and deeper into the abyss of my own despair. I struggle to keep afloat amidst the waves of my memories, but it feels like an endless battle. The more I try to remember, the more I forget, and the weaker I feel.

Every morning I wake up feeling like a new hell is waiting for me. Every day is a repetitive loop of torment—both mental and physical. I am trapped in a monotonous cycle of suffering with no end in sight. This mundane life is a constant painful reminder of the lack of control I have over my own existence.

I feel lost; I don't know where I am, I don't know how long I've been here. All I know is that I miss everyone, I miss who I used to be, I miss my old life. A life that seems like a distant memory.

It seems like a lifetime ago.

Has it been a lifetime?

The world I once knew is now a foreign place. The loneliness is overwhelming.

I feel alone, so alone.

Everyone thinks I died.

Where is everyone?

Where are mom and dad and Marshal and… *Luca*?

Luca, right Luca. He died. I killed him. I didn't kill him. I promise I didn't. Mom and Dad said they hated me. They said I did something bad. I killed their son. Mom said I was a curse, she wished she had aborted me. Mom please don't hate me for killing your son. She said I was mentally ill but Mom I promise I'm fine. I promise I didn't kill him. I didn't kill him; I promise it wasn't my intention. I didn't want to kill him.

I can feel their gaze on me, giving me awful looks, weighing me down with their disapproving stares. Each of them is dressed in pristine white, are the doctors here to diagnose me? Or are they prison guards, here to keep me contained? Where am I?

Is this a sanctuary or a prison? Am I in a place of healing or captivity?

Days meld into one another, time slipping away unnoticed. The hours drag by slowly, it feels torturous. It feels like it's been forever since I've been outside, breathing fresh air and feeling the warmth of the sun but I still remember.

I still remember my dad talking on the phone while we were at the grocery shop.

"We will be sending Krista to you by next week."

Send me where? What did he mean? Is this the place he wanted to send me to?

I remember I was scared, so scared. I ran and ran and ran till I came across a park, and I saw a man. He looked like he was on drugs or a criminal or both, I don't know. He asked me what's wrong I remember I was frantic, I remember I got scared, I ran again then I ran and then I fell.

Everything went black.

Dark

Quiet

I don't remember how I got here but I vaguely remember that I saw mom and dad and the old lady in the white coat talk about me. My mom was crying and my dad continued to talk to her.

She is in good hands.

No one can know about this.

I assure you Mr. and Mrs. Grant we will take great care of her.

Our staff members have been made to sign an NDA, rest assured.

Thanks a lot for the favor Mrs. Cooper.

Don't thank me, It's the least I can do for you after everything you did for me.

Right the lady, she was my doctor, I think. Her name was Barbara Cooper. I heard she's now dead though.

Thank god
Thank God

ABOUT THE AUTHOR

Kaashvi Jain is a 16-year-old girl living in Delhi, India, with her parents, grandparents, and younger sister. She began reading at age 7, starting with children's books like *Thea Stilton* and *Enid Blyton*. Over time, she developed a taste for more suspenseful stories, particularly in the genre of murder mysteries.

While she is passionate about reading and writing, Kaashvi is also interested in other hobbies such as sketching, playing guitar, and listening to music. She often draws inspiration from these activities, incorporating them into her writing, which gives her a unique perspective.

Aside from her hobbies, she is currently a student in the 11th grade at a CBSE-affiliated school in New Delhi.

The Lost Souls is her debut book.

ACKNOWLEDGMENTS

The Lost Souls would have remained just a lost idea in my head without the unwavering support and encouragement I received while writing it.

First and foremost, my deepest gratitude goes to my mentor, Kanchana Banerjee. Her invaluable guidance and insightful feedback were instrumental in shaping the narrative of this book. I am forever grateful for her belief in my vision and for helping me bring Ophelia's story to life.

A heartfelt thanks to Romita Khurana Sahni, author and founder of Avid Readers Club. Her unwavering support and assistance at every step made this book a reality and made the whole process a lot less overwhelming. Without her encouragement, The Lost Souls might never have existed.

I am also immensely grateful to Sagar Azad, founder of Anecdote Publishing House and Champ Readers Private Limited, for providing a platform for my work. To my editor, Meraki, thank you for your meticulous attention to detail and for helping me refine this book to its fullest potential.

I owe a deep debt of gratitude to my parents, Neha Jain and Nikhil Jain, whose constant faith in me pushed me to pursue my passion for writing. Their unwavering support made this journey possible.

To my family, my sister, Aaradhya Jain; my paternal grandparents, Uma Jain and Vinod Kumar Jain; and my maternal grandparents, Anu Jain and Anil Jain—thank you for supporting me in every aspect of life.

Finally, thank you, dear reader, for picking up this book and giving it a chance. I hope you find as much joy in reading *The Lost Souls* as I did in writing it. I also hope this book means as much to you as it does to me.